THE KIDS OF CATTYWAMPUS STREET

LISA JAHN-CLOUGH

Illustrations by Natalie Andrewson

a·s·b

anne schwartz books

Text copyright © 2021 by Lisa Jahn-Clough
Jacket art and interior illustrations copyright © 2021 by Natalie Andrewson

All rights reserved. Published in the United States by Anne Schwartz Books,
an imprint of Random House Children's Books, a division
of Penguin Random House LLC, New York.

Anne Schwartz Books and the colophon are trademarks
of Penguin Random House LLC.

Visit us on the Web! rhcbooks.com

Educators and librarians, for a variety of teaching tools,
visit us at RHTeachersLibrarians.com

Library of Congress Cataloging-in-Publication Data
Names: Jahn-Clough, Lisa, author. | Andrewson, Natalie, illustrator.
Title: The kids of Cattywampus Street / Lisa Jahn-Clough ;
illustrations by Natalie Andrewson.
Description: First edition. | New York : Anne Schwartz Books, [2021] | Audience: Ages
7–10. | Audience: Grades 2–5. | Summary: Eleven stories about the eleven kids who
live on the long and twisty Cattywampus Street out in the middle of Nowheresville.
Identifiers: LCCN 2020027315 | ISBN 978-0-593-12756-8 (hardcover) |
ISBN 978-0-593-12757-5 (library binding) | ISBN 978-0-593-12758-2 (ebook)
Subjects: CYAC: Neighborhoods—Fiction.
Classification: LCC PZ7.J153536 Ki 2021 | DDC [Fic]—dc23

The text of this book is set in 15-point Adobe Jenson Pro.
The illustrations were rendered digitally.
Book design by Michelle Cunningham

Printed in the United States of America
10 9 8 7 6 5 4 3 2 1
First Edition

This book is dedicated to two kids named Ellery and Acadia because they heard a lot of these stories as I was writing them and made many helpful comments! However, they will not be kids forever; therefore, it is also dedicated to the kid who is holding this book in their hands and reading these very words. And that kid is . . . YOU!

—L.J.C.

To every toy store that sparked my imagination

—N.A.

CONTENTS

Charlotta's Apartment

Ameera's House

Hans's House

Pet Store

Ursula's Apartment

PETS

Waddlebee's

STOP

So It Begins . . .

I AM GOING TO TELL YOU SOME STORIES ABOUT THE KIDS who live on Cattywampus Street.

Have you ever traveled there? You'd know if you had. Cattywampus Street is very crooked and twisty, way out in the middle of nowhere. In fact Cattywampus actually means "crooked and not lined up properly." And after the crookedest twist, right before the train tracks, where the pavement ends, is the Waddlebee Toy Store.

The Waddlebee Toy Store has been around as long as anyone can remember. The paint is peeling off the wooden clapboards, a window or two is broken, and the door hangs crooked.

Both inside and outside Waddlebee's and all up and down Cattywampus Street, strange things have been known to happen. . . .

But these stories are not about the toy store or the street. As I said, they are about the kids. The kids' names are Lionel, Lindalee, Hans, Evelyn, Charlotta, Rodney, Mateo, Ameera, Emmett, Bob, and Ursula. Some might seem just like you; others might seem nothing at all like you. You might *wish* you were like these kids, and you might *wish* the things that happen to them could happen to you. On the other hand, you might wish nothing of the sort whatsoever. You'll have to read the stories to see.

You might find these stories odd or mysterious, silly or scary, happy or even sad. But however you find them, I hope you like them. And if you are ever winding along Cattywampus Street and pass the Waddlebee Toy Store, watch out—you just might end up in one of these stories yourself!

The Magic Ball

- THE STORY OF LIONEL -

THIS IS THE FIRST STORY, AND IT IS ABOUT LIONEL.

Lionel lived in the first house on Cattywampus Street. He was a nice boy, a quiet boy, a boy who was easy to get along with. Everybody liked Lionel.

One day Lionel went to buy a magic ball.

Now, you might think it silly to try to buy a magic ball. Maybe you don't believe in magic. But Lionel believed in magic, and he had been saving up for a long, long time to buy a magic ball. Finally, he had enough money.

Lionel walked all the way to the Waddlebee Toy Store at the end of Cattywampus Street, where the pavement ends. The toy store was on the first floor of a two-story building. It had an old sign above the door that said WADDLEBEE in faded red letters. The sign didn't even say it was a toy store, but you could tell it was because of the display in the front window. There were stuffed animals (lions and tigers and bears), a big dollhouse, floppy puppets, squeaky toys, windup toys, toy cars, toy trucks, toy trains, all kinds of puzzles and games, and, yes, some balls.

Lionel opened the door and a tiny little bell went *jing-a-ling-ling.*

The shopkeeper looked up and frowned. She seemed like she was in a bad mood, but Lionel walked over to her anyway.

"Do you have any magic balls?" he asked.

The shopkeeper grumbled something Lionel couldn't understand and pointed to the back of the store.

Lionel walked along the dusty, dark aisles. He passed a stuffed monkey, a plastic squeaky frog, some rubber spiders, and a lot of balls of all different colors and sizes. But none seemed magic. So he kept going.

Finally, in a way, way back corner, on the tippy-top shelf behind a bunch of blocks, was one ball with a bright red star. The star twinkled in the dim light, casting a reddish glow on Lionel's face.

Lionel smiled. This was the magic ball he was looking for!

But the ball was way too high for him to reach. How would he get it down?

He could ask the shopkeeper, but she was busy yelling at another customer and he didn't want to interrupt.

So Lionel started wishing. This is what he wished: *I wish that magic ball would roll off the tippy-top shelf and right into my arms!*

And lo and behold, it did! The magic ball with the bright red star rolled right into Lionel's arms! The red star twinkled.

Lionel brought it to the register.

The other customer had moved on, and now the shopkeeper glared at Lionel over the top of her eyeglasses. "Are you sure you want that silly old ball?" she asked.

"Yes," said Lionel. He paid for it and went on his way.

Outside, he ran into his friends Lindalee and Hans. At least, he *thought* they were his friends, but being around magic can change people, and not always for the best. And in this story, Lindalee and Hans are not so nice, as you will soon see.

"What's that?" asked Lindalee, pointing at the magic ball.

"Yeah, what's that?" asked Hans, pointing, too. He always followed Lindalee.

"It's my new ball," answered Lionel.

"Why does it have a star?" asked Lindalee. She squinted at the star.

"Yeah, why?" echoed Hans. He squinted, too.

"It has a star because it's magic," Lionel told them.

Lindalee reached up and tightened the pink bow in her hair. "What can it do that's magic?" she asked with a gleam in her eye.

"Yeah, what can it do?" Hans asked. He had a gleam in his eye, too, but he didn't have a pink bow to tighten, although he wished he did. He tugged at his shirt collar instead.

Lionel looked at the magic ball. Once again, the red star twinkled. "I'm not sure yet," he said.

Lindalee and Hans nodded at each other. Did they believe Lionel? I don't know, but Lindalee definitely looked like she was up to no good. She may have even winked at Hans behind Lionel's back.

But Lionel paid them no mind. He said goodbye and continued on his way.

Lionel didn't know it, but Lindalee and Hans were following him.

When he got home, Lionel put the magic ball on the top shelf of his closet, then went to his swim lesson. He couldn't very well have taken the magic ball to the pool. What if he dropped it in the water and it lost its magic?

After Lionel was gone, Lindalee walked up to his front door and rang the doorbell. Hans was right next to her.

Lionel's mother answered.

"Lionel said we could play with his ball," Lindalee said. She smiled very sweetly.

"Yeah, he said we could play with it," said Hans. He smiled, too.

Lionel's mother believed them. Why wouldn't she? So she went to Lionel's room and picked up the first ball she saw, a yellow one with stripes. She brought it out. "Here you go," Lionel's mother said.

"No, no, no!" said Lindalee, stomping. "That is the *wrong* ball. Lionel said the ball with the red star."

"Yeah, a bright red star," said Hans. And, yes, he stomped, too.

So Lionel's mother found the ball with the red star in his closet and gave it to Lindalee and Hans. Hans was about to say thank you, but Lindalee grabbed the ball and ran off. How rude! Hans ran after her.

Lindalee and Hans were laughing so hard and running so fast that they forgot to look where they were going. Suddenly Lindalee bumped smack into a telephone pole and—whoops!—she dropped the magic ball.

It rolled into the street. Uh-oh.

"Stupid pole!" yelled Lindalee.

"Stupid pole!" repeated Hans, even though he hadn't bumped into it.

"Stupid ball!" yelled Lindalee when she noticed the ball rolling away.

"Stupid ball!" repeated Hans. Then he added, "I can get it."

Hans was about to chase the ball, when a police officer came out of nowhere and stopped him. "You can't run into the street like that. You might get hurt," said the police officer.

The police officer may have stopped Lindalee and Hans, but he did not stop the magic ball. The ball rolled and rolled. It rolled across Cattywampus Street up onto the sidewalk, and it kept rolling. All the time the red star twinkled, though it could just have been the sunlight.

Now, it so happened that Lionel's swim lesson had been canceled because the instructor had a bad case of swimmer's ear. At that very moment, Lionel was heading home, down that very sidewalk.

And guess what he found?

Yup!

It was his very own magic ball, rolling right toward him. The ball stopped at Lionel's feet and bobbled back and forth, as if it were excited. The red star twinkled extra bright.

Lionel picked it up. "Wow—my magic ball knew just where I was," he said.

Then he noticed Lindalee and Hans on the other side of the street. They did not look happy.

The police officer was still there. It looked like he was giving them a lecture.

Lionel waved to his friends. They did not wave back, which he thought was a little odd, but he didn't mind.

After all, Lionel finally had a magic ball.

Jing-a-ling-ling.

The Mean Girl

- THE STORY OF LINDALEE -

AS YOU MAY HAVE GUESSED FROM THE PREVIOUS STORY, Lindalee was a mean girl.

Hopefully, you have never met a girl as mean as Lindalee. And if you have, I am sorry.

Lindalee was mean all the time—at school, at the playground, even at birthday parties. She was mean to her teachers, her friends, and strangers. Lindalee lived in a first-floor apartment on Cattywampus Street with her grandmother, Nana Gigi, and believe it or not, she was even mean to her!

That's right—Lindalee was a downright mean machine.

Lindalee didn't know why she was mean. She would want to be nice, she would plan to be nice, she would *try* to be nice, but at the very last minute a little voice in her head would say, *BE MEAN!*

And so she would be. She couldn't help it.

You might wonder how Lindalee had any friends. Well, she never had them for long. As soon as Hans, or Lionel, or Charlotta, or Evelyn and Emmett, or any of the other kids found out how mean Lindalee could be, they no longer wanted to be around her.

By and by, there came a day when there was no one left for her to be friends with.

On that day, Lindalee walked home from school all alone. It was a beautiful day. Not a cloud was in the sky. The sun was shining, but Lindalee hated the sun.

"Sun," she yelled, "you are hot! You are stupid! And you are ugly, too!" (What a mean thing to say to the sun!)

Suddenly a big gray cloud covered the sun and it started to rain.

"Oh, no!" Lindalee cried. She hated the rain just as much as she hated the sun.

"Rain," she yelled, "you are wet! You are stupid! And you are ugly, too!" (What a mean thing to say to the rain!)

Lindalee walked faster, as if that would keep her dry. But the rain just came down harder and she just got wetter.

Lindalee started to run. She ran right by her own apartment, then the park, then the Waddlebee Toy Store, and finally across the train tracks. She ran and ran and ran, until—oops!—she slipped in the mud and fell into a deep puddle.

Down, down, down, and down she fell . . . until—*ka-thunk!*—Lindalee landed. Her pretty pink dress was covered with slime.

"Oh, no! My dress is ruined!" she yelled.

Her pretty white shoes were also covered with slime.

"Oh, no! My shoes are ruined!" she yelled.

And right there in the mud, Lindalee started to cry. Big, fat tears streamed down her muddy face. "Boo-hoo! Boo-hoo-hoo!"

"What's your problem?" a grubby, groggy voice asked.

Where was that voice coming from? Lindalee dried her tears and looked around. Nobody was in front of her, nobody was next to her, and nobody was behind her.

"Wh-wh-who's that?" she stuttered.

"Down here," said the grubby, groggy voice.

"Where?" asked Lindalee. She moved onto the wet grass.

"Watch it! You almost sat on me, you ninny!" the voice yelled.

Lindalee peered down and saw a grubby, groggy

tiny frog right next to her, almost buried in the muddy grass. *A frog can't talk,* she thought. *Can it?*

"Yeah. It's me, silly," the frog said. "A FROG!" The frog stretched itself up straight, warts and all.

"Eww! You're gross! And ugly!" Lindalee screamed.

"And you are mean, mean, mean, MEAN!" the frog screamed right back. "That's why you have NO friends, and that's why you're sitting here all alone, feeling sorry for yourself. Your dress is stupid and ugly, that ribbon in your hair is ridiculous. I've never seen such hideous shoes before in my life. . . ." The frog went on and on and on, pointing out everything it thought was stupid and ugly. Which, trust me, was a lot.

Lindalee couldn't stand it. This was the meanest frog ever!

Lindalee was so upset that she got up and started running. She ran and ran, back across the train

tracks to Cattywampus Street. As she passed the toy store, her dress became dry and pretty again. Her shoes were no longer dirty. The sun came out and the clouds rolled away.

Lindalee ran all the way home. When she got there, she ran up to her grandmother and hugged her. "You are the best, Nana!" she cried. "I love you so much!"

"Do I know you?" Nana Gigi replied.

"It is me, Lindalee!" Lindalee said.

Nana Gigi shook her head. "I don't think so."

Next, Lindalee ran to the school, where her teacher, Mr. Belloc, was just leaving. "I love you so much!" she yelled. "I love school, too!"

"Who are you?" Mr. Belloc asked.

"It is me, Lindalee!" Lindalee said.

"No," said Mr. Belloc. "That's not possible."

Lindalee went to see all her former friends. First Hans, then Lionel, then Charlotta, then Emmett and Evelyn, and so on. One by one, she hugged them and told them how much she loved them. And one by one, they asked who she was.

"It is *me*, Lindalee!" Lindalee said over and over. But no one believed her.

Lindalee went back to her house. This time Nana Gigi wouldn't even let her in. "Sorry," she said. "You look like a nice girl. But I miss my mean Lindalee."

Lindalee sat on the stoop and tried to think of ways she could prove that she was indeed the real Lindalee. Then she heard that little voice in her head again. Not the grubby, groggy frog voice, but the familiar voice.

BE MEAN, it said.

Lindalee tightened her pink bow so tight her head hurt, then stood up and took a big breath. "OPEN UP AND LET ME IN!" she shouted in her loudest, meanest voice. "Everyone is so stupid—you don't even know that it is me, Lindalee!"

Nana Gigi opened the door. "Here's my Lindalee!"

She was so happy to have Lindalee back that she gave her a big bowl of strawberry ice cream and a chewy chocolate chip cookie.

And Lindalee was never nice again, except every once in a while when she couldn't help it.

Yippee!

Waffles for Breakfast

- THE STORY OF HANS -

WHEN HANS WOKE TO THE SCRUMPTIOUS SMELL OF HOT, fresh waffles baking, he thought it was the most perfect morning. Because everybody loves waffles, right? Well, Hans really, really, REALLY loved them!

Mmm, my lovely mommy is making my favorite breakfast, Hans thought. Hans was very lucky to have a lovely mommy who often made his favorite breakfast. We should all be so lucky. But sometimes we are not as lucky as we think we are. . . .

Hans put on his favorite robot T-shirt and a pink hair bow that Lindalee had given him once when she was being nice. His mouth watered as he walked down the stairs, just thinking of the crisp, buttery waffles dripping with maple syrup. Yum, yum, yum.

When he got to the kitchen, there was his lovely mommy setting the table just for him. "Good morning, lovely Hans, darling," she said.

"Good morning, lovely Mommy, darling," said Hans. "You sound strange."

And in fact, her voice did seem different. Scratchier or something.

"Oh, Hans, darling, I just have a little cold. *Achoo!*" She rubbed her nose and achooed again. "See?"

"A little cold?" Hans asked. "Do you need to go back to bed?"

His lovely mommy laughed. "Oh, Hans, you are too sweet, but I do not need to go back to bed. I am here to serve you breakfast."

And Hans believed her, even though she hadn't

even noticed how nice he looked in his robot T-shirt and hair bow.

"Are you ready for waffles?" she asked.

"YES, I am ready for waffles!" said Hans. Then he added "please" and "thank you" because he was, after all, sweet.

His mommy put a plate of fresh waffles in front of him. Hans smothered them with butter and syrup. He took a bite.

DELICIOUS!

Hans gobbled them all up lickety-split.

"My, my," his mommy said. "You are quite the hungry boy. Would you like some more?"

"YES!" said Hans, and then he added, "Please and thank you!"

And so his lovely mommy placed another plate of fresh waffles in front of him. And again Hans smothered them with butter and syrup and gobbled them all up. And again they were DELICIOUS.

"More?" asked his mommy.

"YES!" said Hans. "Please and thank you."

For the third time, his lovely mommy placed a plate of fresh waffles in front of him.

And guess what? Yup. Hans smothered them with butter and syrup and gobbled them all up. And yup, they were DELICIOUS.

"More?" asked his lovely mommy.

"YES!" said Hans. "Please and thank you."

It went on like this for a long time. Hans was a waffle-eating machine, and his lovely mommy was a waffle-making machine to match.

How many waffles do you think Hans ate?

Ten?

No. It was more than that.

Twenty?

No. More than that.

Thirty?

Nope. Keep counting.

Forty?

Fifty?

Sixty?

Seventy?

Nope, nope, nope, and nope.

It was more than eighty and even more than ninety!

Hans ate ONE HUNDRED waffles that morning. All of them smothered in butter and syrup, and all of them DELICIOUS. In fact, each waffle was better than the one before.

But finally, after the one hundredth waffle, Hans was stuffed. His belly was so full it hurt.

"Don't you want any more waffles?" his lovely mommy asked.

"No, thank you," groaned Hans.

"But you must eat one more," she said. "I have been making them all morning just for you."

Now, here is where I should warn you that this

lovely mommy was not Hans's real mommy. She was a fake mommy, and she was not lovely at all, as you will soon see. But she looked just like his mommy, and she acted just like his mommy, and she was exactly like his mommy in every way . . . except for her strange voice (but she had a cold, right?), so Hans was sure she was his mommy.

Hans thought his mommy was so lovely to make him so many yummy waffles that he didn't want to disappoint her. So even though he was really, *really* full, Hans said he would eat just one more. After all, it was the polite thing to do.

Hans's (fake) mommy put the last waffle in front of him. The butter was perfectly melted. The sugary syrup trickled into the crispy nooks. He took a bite. This time more slowly, because he was so full.

"Eat up, Hans, darling," his (fake) mommy said. "You mustn't let good food go to waste."

Hans forced down one more bite and then

another and another. Each went into his mouth, down his throat, and into his very full, very stuffed belly, which stretched out even more.

Finally, there was just one last bite of waffle left on his plate. Hans speared it with his fork and put it on his tongue. He closed his mouth, then chewed and swallowed with a big gulp. Down it went!

Hans was now so full of waffle that he was more waffle than boy. He smelled like waffle. He looked like waffle.

He was so much like waffle that his lovely (fake) mommy, who by now was very, very hungry herself, smiled a not-very-lovely smile and told Hans, "I am not your lovely mommy! I hid your lovely mommy in the closet! And I am HUNGRY!"

Then she smothered Hans with butter and syrup and she gobbled him up, lickety-split!

And wouldn't you know, Hans *tasted* just like waffle, too.

But remember that Hans had eaten one hundred waffles, plus that last one, which made one hundred and one.

So when his not-very-lovely fake mommy ate him, she also ate all those waffles inside of him. She started to feel sick, because even though she loved waffles, there is such a thing as too many waffles.

Her stomach twisted and gurgled. Her throat tickled and she let out a little burp. Then she let out a big burp, and then . . . she threw up. Blech! She threw up all one hundred and one waffles—it was a lot of throw-up. Then, finally, I must tell you, she threw up Hans. Right onto the floor.

Hans jumped to his feet, wiped himself off, and chased that mean fake mommy out of the house. "You get out of here and never come back!" he shouted.

Hans chased her all the way to the end of Cattywampus Street, where she ran straight into the Waddlebee Toy Store and was never seen again.

When Hans got home, he found his real mommy, his lovely mommy, stuck in the closet behind an old trunk and some moth-eaten sweaters. He let her out. They hugged and hugged.

Then his real mommy said, "You look lovely this morning, Hans! Do you want some waffles for breakfast?"

Hans shook his head. "Thank you, but no thank you, lovely Mommy. I don't like waffles anymore."

And after that, his real mommy never, ever made waffles for breakfast again.

Yum, yum.

A Very, Very, Very Sad Story

- THE STORY OF EVELYN -

I WARN YOU: THIS IS GOING TO BE A SAD STORY. IT WILL GET sadder and sadder as it goes on. The end will be okay, but still, you might cry.

It is about Evelyn, who lived in a yellow house on Cattywampus Street with her mother; her father; her brother, Emmett; and her cat, Chocolate Bear. She loved them all very much. Sometimes her brother wasn't very nice to her, but she still loved him.

Evelyn liked to do things with her family, with her friends, and by herself.

Here are some of the things she liked to do with

her family: have picnics in the park, go to the zoo, bake coconut cookies (and eat them), and just hang out.

Here are some of the things she liked to do with her friends: take bike rides, swim in the pool, go to the toy store, and just hang out.

And here are some things she liked to do by herself: read fairy tales, play "Für Elise" on the piano, cuddle with Chocolate Bear, and make up stories.

So far everything in this story is happy, especially Evelyn. But no one can be happy all the time. I mean, are YOU always happy? I don't think so. Sometimes you are sad. And sometimes Evelyn was sad, too. Sometimes she even *liked* being sad. In fact, one of her favorite things to do, besides all the stuff already listed, was to sit under the willow tree in the park and think sad thoughts.

One day as she sat under the willow tree, Evelyn heard a rustle in the bushes. It sounded just like

Chocolate Bear when he was playing around outside. *Rustle, rustle, rustle.*

"Here, kitty, kitty," Evelyn called. But Chocolate Bear didn't come running and meowing the way he usually did. She looked under the bush, but she didn't see him. She crawled deeper into the bush . . . and there he was, lying very still.

"Come here, sweetie-weetie, kitty-witty, Chocolate Bear!" Evelyn said, but Chocolate Bear didn't move.

Evelyn reached out and touched his body. It was cold and stiff. She put her hand where his heart was and there was no beat.

"Oh, no! Chocolate Bear is dead!" cried Evelyn.

Now, this is sad, but it is not the saddest part of this very, very, very sad story.

Evelyn tried to move poor Chocolate Bear, but his body was tangled in the prickers. She ran home to get her parents, crying all the way. Just as she

reached the front door, her father opened it. She was about to tell him that Chocolate Bear was dead, when she noticed he was already crying.

"What's wrong?" asked Evelyn.

"Emmett i-i-is . . . d-d-d-dead!" Evelyn's father cried.

"What?! NO! He can't be dead!" Evelyn burst into tears. First her cat, now her brother.

Her father told Evelyn that Emmett had been chasing a ball across Cattywampus Street when a car drove by and hit him. An ambulance had taken him to the hospital, but it was too late.

Now, this is very sad, but it is still not the saddest part of this very, very, very sad story.

Both Evelyn and her father sat on the step and cried and cried and cried. Then Evelyn asked where her mother was. Why wasn't she there, too?

"Well," her father said, "she was so sad, she had to go to the zoo, where she likes to cry."

So Evelyn and her father went to the zoo to find her mother.

They passed the penguins waddling and splashing into the water. Her mother wasn't there.

They passed the monkeys swinging on the branches, going "chee-chee-chee," but her mother wasn't there, either.

When they got to the lions' section, there was a big crowd and everybody was screaming.

"What's wrong?" Evelyn asked the zookeeper.

"A woman fell over the wall into the den and was eaten by the lion!" the zookeeper said.

And do you know what? I have to tell you that the woman who was eaten by the lion was none other than . . . you guessed it, Evelyn's mother.

"OH, NO!!!" Evelyn cried.

"OH, NO!!!" her father cried.

How could they go on?

But even though this is very, very sad, it is

STILL not the saddest part of this very, very, very
sad story.

Evelyn and her father went back home, crying
the whole time. And do you know what sad thing
happened next? On their way, Evelyn's father tripped
and he cracked his head, and . . . yes, he died, too!

How could this ever be? Now Evelyn had no one.
First her cat, then her brother, then her mother,
then her father. What next?

Evelyn stumbled the rest of the way home all
alone. She cried and cried. She didn't even see her
friends Ameera and Rodney across the street. They
waved to her, but Evelyn was too busy crying and
crying and crying and crying.

It seemed like she would cry forever.

The good news is, that was the last sad part
of this very, very, very sad story. (I told you it was
going to be sad, didn't I?)

But wait, the story is not over! As Evelyn cried,

she thought she heard a faint rustle. She opened her eyes and listened. There it was again. *Rustle, rustle, rustle,* followed by a little "mew." Evelyn wiped away her tears and looked in the bushes.

Chocolate Bear came running out. He wasn't dead!

Evelyn picked him up and cuddled him. She carried him home, and guess what? Emmett was there. He wasn't dead! And her mother and her father were there, too. Nobody was dead! Evelyn had just been imagining all these very, very, very sad things.

Evelyn hugged everybody (even her brother).

And to make herself feel better, she went down to the Waddlebee Toy Store. This time she saw Lionel kicking his magic ball, and Lindalee, who actually smiled. Then Evelyn bought a stuffed lion with her allowance, and even the grumpy shopkeeper smiled.

Back home, Evelyn set the lion on top of her piano and played "Für Elise" six times. Then her family made coconut cookies together and ate them!

Evelyn was overjoyed that everyone was still alive, but when she remembered all of those sad thoughts, she felt very, very, very sad again, and she cried a little more. She didn't want anyone to die.

And now it really is the end of this story.

Boo-hoo. Boo-hoo-hoo.

The Happily-
Ever-After House

- THE STORY OF CHARLOTTA -

TO MAKE UP FOR THAT LAST STORY, I WILL TELL YOU A HAPPY ONE.

Charlotta had five dolls—a mommy doll, a daddy doll, a girl doll, a boy doll, and a baby doll.

Oh, yes, and a dog doll, too! So that makes six.

The dolls were made of wood, and they were so well loved and well played with that their painted faces were faded and strands of their yarn hair were missing. The dog's yarn fur was almost completely gone. Their clothes were made of tiny pieces of rags. The dog, of course, didn't have clothes, but he had a tiny, faded blue ribbon for a collar.

The doll family lived in a shoe box next to

Charlotta's bed. She didn't have enough money to buy a real dollhouse. (This may seem sad, but the story is not over yet. Just wait.)

Every day after school, Charlotta walked down Cattywampus Street to the Waddlebee Toy Store and stared at the big dollhouse in the window.

My dolls would love that house, she thought.

One day Charlotta packed up her dolls in their shoe box and carried them to the toy store. In front of the window, she lifted the lid of the shoe box just enough for her dolls to see the big, beautiful dollhouse.

Charlotta wasn't entirely sure, but she was pretty sure that she heard her dolls gasp with delight. How beautiful the house was! So many rooms! There was a big bedroom for the parents with a four-poster bed! A bedroom for the boy and girl with a bunk bed! A nursery for the baby with a rocking crib! There was even a fancy, fluffy bed for the dog! And there were all kinds of extra rooms for guests to come and stay whenever they wanted! The living room had a fireplace with a mantel and candlesticks! There was a tiny piano with real keys that could be played! And in the kitchen there was a table, and on the table was a yummy doll cake! Charlotta thought it looked like chocolate—her favorite!

"Someday I am going to buy this house for you," Charlotta told her dolls.

Charlotta saved and saved and saved every penny she could. She did chores for the neighbors. She searched for change on the sidewalk and in the park, just in case. But the dollhouse cost a lot of money, and it was going to take Charlotta a long, long time to save that much. She visited the dollhouse every day, then hurried home to tell her dolls it was still there.

But one day when Charlotta went to see the

dollhouse . . . it was gone! She opened the door of the Waddlebee Toy Store and the bell went *jing-a-ling-ling.* She went up to the shopkeeper and asked where the dollhouse was.

"What dollhouse? I don't know what you're talking about," she grumbled.

"There was a big, beautiful dollhouse in the window!" cried Charlotta.

"Well, it's gone now," the shopkeeper said.

There was nothing Charlotta could do but go home and break the bad news to her dolls.

Does this still seem sad? Well, it's not anymore, because when Charlotta got to her room, instead of the shoe box, guess what she found?

The very dollhouse from the toy store! Her dolls were in it—sitting in the living room in little, comfy armchairs, having a tea party. The dog was snuggled in the fluffy dog bed by the fireplace.

How did the dollhouse get there?

Could Charlotta's parents have snuck out and bought it when Charlotta was sleeping?

Could it have gotten there by magic?

Well, however it got there, there it was. And the dolls had moved right in.

They must like it, Charlotta thought.

And they did. They liked it a lot.

As Charlotta watched, the daddy doll started playing the piano and the other dolls began dancing! The dog doll wagged its tail and jumped about.

Charlotta wanted so badly to join them. She especially wanted a bite of the yummy doll cake that was on the table in the kitchen. She wanted to know if it was indeed chocolate.

You see, I didn't tell you this yet, but Charlotta's own house was pretty small and bare. She had to share a room with her little brother, Chadwick, and her baby sister, Charlena. Her grandparents slept in the other bedroom and her parents slept on a foldout bed in the living room. Her family could not afford comfy armchairs, let alone a piano. They usually had cabbage for supper and never, ever had chocolate cake.

Sad again? Please, keep reading—the best part is *still* coming, I promise.

Just then, Charlotta's brother and sister wailed from the living room and her mother yelled at them to settle down, and then her grandfather grumbled loudly from his bedroom.

Charlotta covered her ears, squeezed her eyes shut tight, and took a deep breath. Slowly, she reached out her left hand and put it in the dollhouse.

When Charlotta opened her eyes, her hand had gotten smaller!

Her baby sister gave another wail, and Charlotta put in her entire left arm. Believe it or not, her entire left arm got smaller!

She put in her right arm and hand, her left foot, then her right foot, and she got small enough that she could squeeze her whole self right into the dollhouse.

Now all of Charlotta was inside the house. She had shrunk enough so that she fit perfectly.

"Hello!" she said to the doll family.

"Hello!" the doll family said.

"Wah, wah," said the doll baby.

"Woof, woof!" said the doll dog. Charlotta gave it a pat.

"We're so happy you're here," said the doll daddy.

"We've been waiting for you," said the doll mommy.

"Play with us!" said the doll girl and boy.

Charlotta played with the dolls all day. They had the most wonderful time. When they were done, the doll mommy and the doll daddy said, "Now we have a surprise for you!"

Can you guess what it was? They brought out the yummy doll cake and put little doll candles in it, even though it wasn't Charlotta's birthday.

"This is to thank you for getting us this beautiful house," the doll daddy said.

"But I didn't," Charlotta explained. "I don't even know how it got here."

"Don't you see?" said the doll mommy. "You wished for it, and here it is."

"Just like you wished to come play with us, and you did," said the doll boy and girl. "You must be very magic."

The doll baby said, "Wah, wah, magic," and the doll dog said, "Woof, woof, magic."

Charlotta wasn't sure if it was magic, but then of course here she was, inside the dollhouse.

Whether Charlotta was magic or not, she was very happy.

The dolls served up the doll cake. And do you know what kind of cake it was?

YES! It was chocolate. And it *was* yummy indeed.

And that's the happily-ever-after ending.

But not quite. It gets even better.

Remember how Charlotta's own house was small and she had to share a room with her little brother and baby sister and her grandparents slept in the other room and her parents could only afford cabbage for supper? Well, Charlotta squeezed her eyes really tight and wished really hard.

When she opened her eyes, there were her parents, her grandparents, her little brother, and her baby sister inside the dollhouse.

So Charlotta and her family all lived together with the doll family in the big, beautiful dollhouse with plenty of room for all, and plenty of cake, too.

And *that* is how Charlotta really, truly lived happily ever after.

Wah, wah. Woof, woof.

A Perfect Pet

- THE STORY OF RODNEY -

ALL OF RODNEY'S FRIENDS HAD PETS.

Lionel had a boa constrictor.

Charlotta had a cheetah.

Ameera had an aardvark.

Even Mateo, who liked to do nothing, had a monkey.

Rodney wanted a pet, too. He wanted a pet to cuddle and hold, to play with when he was lonely, and to comfort him when he got scared, especially at night. Rodney had a mama and a mommy who both loved him very much, but they couldn't always be there to comfort him, and Rodney didn't like to complain.

Finally, he mustered up the courage to ask them, "Can I have a pet?"

His mama sighed. "I'm sorry, Rodney, but we live in a small apartment."

"But Lionel, Charlotta, Ameera, and Mateo have pets," Rodney said.

His mommy shook her head. "Pets are messy and loud. The neighbors wouldn't approve. Besides, it's against the building rules."

"What about a fish?" asked Rodney.

His mama and mommy looked at each other.

"A fish might be okay," said his mama.

"We can pick one out together," said his mommy.

"Hooray!" said Rodney.

They all walked downstairs. They never took the elevator because it was old and dangerous—there had been a terrible accident on it once. Then they headed to the pet store, which happened to be right next to the Waddlebee Toy Store on Catty-wampus Street.

"Are you sure you don't want a toy instead?" Rodney's mama asked, while his mommy pointed to a rubber fish in the toy store window.

"I'm sure," Rodney said. "I want a real, live pet that I can talk to."

They went into the pet store. It was a strange pet store, because there were no dogs or cats or bunnies like you'd expect—just tiny animals, like bugs and fish. Rodney went to the fish tank and picked out an orange one with blue spots.

Rodney and his mama and mommy went home and put the fish in a glass bowl in his room.

That night Rodney watched his fish swim around and around. Around and around and around and around and around. It was boring, so he went to bed.

During the night Rodney had a scary dream. It's

not important to know what it was about, only that it was so scary that Rodney woke up screaming. He needed a hug. He looked at his fish. It was still swimming around.

Eventually, both his moms came in and hugged him.

After that, Rodney felt better, but he frowned at his fish. "You're not a very good pet," he said.

The next day at the park, Rodney told his friends he had a fish.

"Can your fish slither and wrap itself around your neck, like my boa?" asked Lionel.

"Can your fish run as fast as the wind, like my cheetah?" asked Charlotta.

"Can your fish grunt and eat ants, like my anteater?" sang Ameera, who liked to sing.

"Can your fish climb trees and eat bananas, like my monkey?" asked Mateo. Then he added, "Chee-chee-chee!"

"No," said Rodney. "But it can swim around and around."

"BORING!" his friends said.

Rodney sat by himself under the willow tree. He wished he had a pet that could do something, a pet he could cuddle, a pet he could play with and talk to and take with him wherever he went.

Rodney got up and wandered down Cattywampus Street, wishing all the way. He stood in front of the Waddlebee Toy Store, but he still didn't go in. He didn't want a toy—he wanted a better pet. He didn't go into the pet store, either, because they only had bugs and fish, and he already had a fish, and what kind of a pet is a bug anyway?

He headed back to the park. All of a sudden, his foot hit something on the sidewalk and he tripped. "OW!" Rodney said.

Next to his foot was a rock. It wasn't big, but it wasn't small, either. Rodney picked it up. It was a perfect, oval-shaped, medium-sized rock—very smooth and pretty. He cradled it in his palm and rubbed it with his thumb.

Rodney slipped the rock into his pocket, where it fit perfectly.

Back home, Rodney watched his fish swim around and around. When he was totally bored— which, trust me, happened in about ten seconds—he took the rock out of his pocket. It had two little black spots on it. Rodney got a black magic marker and made the spots bigger. Now they looked like eyes.

He got a red magic marker and drew a curved line below the eyes, so the rock looked like it was smiling at him. Rodney smiled back.

"I will call you Rocky," he told the rock.

Rodney wasn't sure, but he thought the rock nodded. He slipped Rocky back into his pocket.

That night, after Rodney said good night to his

moms and to his fish, he held Rocky in his hand and whispered, "Good night, Rocky."

He wasn't sure, but he thought he heard the rock whisper back very softly, "Good night, Rodney."

Rodney held Rocky to his ear and listened again, but he was stone silent. Rodney patted Rocky and tucked him under the pillow.

In the middle of the night, Rodney had another scary dream. This one had a ghost and a knife and it was indeed very scary.

Rodney was about to yell for his moms, when he remembered Rocky under his pillow. He took him out and rubbed his smooth surface and looked into his black eyes. Rocky's smile seemed to grow bigger.

Rodney held Rocky to his ear and was pretty sure he heard the faintest whisper: "Don't be afraid."

Suddenly, Rodney felt better. He didn't need to call for a hug, and he slept soundly for the rest of the night.

The next day, Rodney brought Rocky to school and kept him snug in his pocket. At the park, Rodney showed Rocky to his friends.

"That is a rock," Lionel said.

"It is smiling," said Charlotta.

"And it has eyes," sang Ameera.

"What does it do?" asked Mateo.

"My rock smiles all the time. My rock is smooth. My rock is named Rocky. Rocky goes everywhere with me," said Rodney. "He keeps me company and is not afraid of anything!"

Rodney demonstrated how Rocky nestled in the palm of his hand, how to rub Rocky's smooth back, and how Rocky went everywhere with him in his pocket.

"I want a rock," said Lionel.

"Me too!" said Charlotta, Ameera, and Mateo all at once.

"What about your pets?" asked Rodney.

"I lied. I don't really have a boa constrictor," said Lionel.

"I don't really have a cheetah," said Charlotta.

"La-la-la, I don't really have an aardvark," sang Ameera.

"But I DO have a monkey! Chee-chee-chee!" said Mateo. (Was Mateo telling the truth? If you read the story about him, maybe you'll know.)

"We can all have rocks!" Rodney said. He helped his friends search the park until they each found a rock.

"My rock is heavy," said Lionel.

"My rock is round," said Charlotta.

"My rock is sharp," sang Ameera.

"My rock has spots all over," said Mateo.

"Our rocks are perfect!" said Lionel, Charlotta, Ameera, Mateo, and Rodney all at the same time.

From then on, all five friends carried their rocks everywhere they went.

Rodney still fed and watched his fish. He even gave it a name—Fishy. Sometimes he let Rocky sit at the bottom of Fishy's bowl. Rocky always smiled, no matter what.

And sometimes at night when Rodney got scared, he was pretty sure that he could hear his rock whisper, "Don't be afraid," and Rodney always felt better.

Zzzzz. . . .

Silly Little Monkey

- THE STORY OF MATEO -

LIKE A LOT OF KIDS, MATEO DID MANY THINGS. IN FACT, HE DID more than most. He played the ukulele, the drums, and the piccolo. He played soccer, practiced ballet, and ran track. He was in the chess club, the math club, and the drama club. He knew thirteen different card games, read all kinds of books, and drew comics. He rode his bike, went to the zoo, and hung out with friends in the park. He told jokes, mixed potions, and built model rockets that he bought from the Waddlebee Toy Store. Phew! That's a lot of things.

But do you know what his favorite thing was? Well, I happen to know that Mateo's favorite thing to do was nothing. Unfortunately, he had very little time to do nothing because he was so busy doing all those other things.

Finally, one day he told his father, "I am going to do nothing all day!"

At first his father was upset because he didn't want Mateo to miss ballet practice, math club, or Lindalee's birthday party.

But Mateo begged and begged. "Please. I really, really, *really* want to do nothing!"

So his father said okay.

Now, where was Mateo going to do nothing?

First he went to his room. But there were so many things there—books, toys, puzzles, games—that Mateo knew he couldn't possibly do nothing with all that stuff around.

So he went outside. He saw his friends Emmett and Rodney riding their bikes. They each had a present in their basket. They stopped when they saw Mateo.

"We're going to Lindalee's party," Emmett told him.

"Are you going?" asked Rodney.

Mateo almost hopped on his bike to go with them, but then he remembered he was busy. "I can't," he said. "I'm doing nothing today."

"Have fun!" Emmett and Rodney called as they rode off.

Mateo crossed Cattywampus Street and went into the park. He had lived across from the park his entire life, so he knew just where to go. At the farthest edge, near the railroad tracks, under the willow tree was a huge rock. This was Mateo's favorite rock. It was twice as big as him and it was very smooth, with a curve that made the perfect comfortable spot to stretch out on his back.

Mateo lay on that rock and did nothing. It was so much fun!

But after a while of doing nothing, Mateo's

stomach grumbled. He was hungry. It was almost lunchtime.

I wish I had a banana, he thought. Bananas were his favorite food. Everybody loves bananas.

Just then something swished in the willow tree above him. Mateo looked up. You will never believe what he saw. There was a little brown monkey with a long, stripy tail. It held something in its hands, but was jumping so fast Mateo couldn't see what it was.

"Wowza!" said Mateo, sitting upright. "You look like a monkey!" He sniffed. "And you smell like one, too."

This silly little monkey grinned. Its stripy tail swished back and forth. "Chee-chee-chee," it said in a silly monkey voice.

The monkey held out the things it was holding— two long yellow things, one in each hand.

Do you know what they were?

Exactly!

Bananas.

That silly little monkey had two bananas.

"Chee-chee-chee," said the monkey, and it shinnied down the tree branch, sat next to Mateo, and waved the bananas at him.

"I was just wishing for a banana," Mateo said. "Can I have one?" After all, the monkey had two, so it could spare one, right? He reached out his hand, then added, "Please."

The monkey looked at one banana, then the other. Then it looked at Mateo and stuck out its tongue.

"Chee-chee-chee," it said. Then that silly little monkey hopped off the rock and scurried away lickety-split.

Mateo remembered he was supposed to be doing nothing, but he really wanted one of those bananas. So he stopped doing nothing, hopped off the rock, and ran after the monkey.

Mateo was good at running. So was the monkey. They ran around the rock, around the park, all the way down Cattywampus Street to the Waddlebee Toy Store, and all the way back to the willow tree.

"Chee-chee-chee!" the monkey said as he scurried up the tree, then tiptoed out along a long, wobbly branch.

It so happened that another thing Mateo was good at was tree climbing. So when the monkey climbed up, Mateo did not hesitate. He scurried up right after the monkey.

The monkey stood at the end of the wobbly branch, bouncing up and down. "Chee-chee-chee!" it teased, waving one of the bananas at Mateo.

And with that, the monkey peeled it, took one bite, then another, and another, until he'd eaten the whole thing. Nothing was left but the peel.

The monkey waved the remaining banana at Mateo.

Mateo could see that banana. He could smell that banana. But this monkey was really starting to annoy him with all its silly monkey antics.

So Mateo inched along the wobbly branch, closer and closer, and reached out his hand so far that he could almost touch the banana. The branch swayed under his weight. Whoa.

Suddenly, the monkey jumped up and down, screaming, "Chee, chee, chee, chee, chee, chee!" about a hundred times. The branch swung all over the place, but the monkey held on with his feet and his long, stripy tail. Then the monkey threw the peel from the first banana at Mateo.

It landed on the branch right in front of him, just as Mateo was taking another step.

Guess what happened?

Yup. *WHOOSH!* Mateo slipped on the banana peel and the branch snapped and—CRACK—he tumbled down to the ground. Luckily, he missed the rock, but he rolled down the grassy knoll to the bottom, where he fell into a mud puddle. *SPLASH!*

The monkey grinned as it jumped to a higher branch and screamed, "BAAA-NAAA-NAAA!" super loud.

Then that silly little monkey threw the other banana right at Mateo. It bonked him on the head and landed with a plop in the mud puddle. A tiny frog went, "Ribbit, ribbit," and hopped away.

Mateo picked up the banana and peeled it. One, two, three bites—he ate the whole thing.

When he was done, Mateo got up and brushed himself off. He looked around, but the monkey had disappeared back whence it came (wherever that was).

The day was almost over, so Mateo headed home. He saw Emmett and Rodney riding toward him.

"How was the party?" Mateo asked.

"It was canceled," Emmett said.

"Lindalee was being rude," Rodney added.

Mateo was pleased that he had missed it. He didn't like it when Lindalee was rude. Even though, now that he thought about it, that monkey had been kind of rude. Or was it just being silly? After all, Mateo had gotten a banana, just as he had wished.

When he got home, his father greeted him. "How was your day doing nothing?" he asked.

"Pretty good," said Mateo. "I met a monkey in the park who gave me a banana."

"That's nice," said his father. "Are you going to do nothing tomorrow, too?" he asked.

"Maybe," said Mateo. "If I have the time."

And with that, he went upstairs, took out one of his model rockets, and got back to work.

Chee-chee-chee!

The Loveliest Song

- THE STORY OF AMEERA -

AMEERA LIVED ON A FARM WITH A DOG, A CAT, A PARROT, ONE horse, two cows, three pigs, four goats, and a lot of chickens. Oh, yes, and her much older sister, who took care of her.

Years ago, when Ameera was a baby, she and Big Sister had lived with their family in a top-floor apartment in town, but sadly, her parents died in an unfortunate elevator accident. After that, Ameera and Big Sister moved to the farm. Together, they did all the chores—cleaned the house, cooked the meals, tended the garden, and fed the animals.

Their farm was on the top of a steep hill, at the end of Cattywampus Street, way past the

Waddlebee Toy Store. Everyone thought the toy store was at the end of the street, but it was only at the end of the paved part. The dirt path to Ameera's was so steep and bumpy that no cars or buses could get up it. So she had to walk to school and back, which took an hour each way.

On the day that this story begins, Ameera skipped down the path, feeling cheerful because it was a cheerful kind of morning. As she passed the toy store, she began to sing. This is what she sang:

La-la-la-la-la-la-la.
What a little song I sing.
La-la-la-la-la-la-la.
A pretty little song fit for a king.
La-la-la-la-la-la-la.

When Ameera got to school, she went straight to her classroom, sat in her chair in the back row, and kept singing. Mr. Belloc told her to be quiet and listen to the lesson, so she stopped for a minute. But then she started again, very softly so no one could hear.

Ameera sang quietly all through science, math, and history.

During story time, Mr. Belloc read a fairy tale about a king in a magic kingdom who needed to have the field plowed in order to do the planting. The king announced a contest to see who could plow the field the fastest. Whoever won would marry the princess and live in the kingdom. There were three brothers who tried. The first two were selfish and greedy, and they failed. The third brother was clever and kind, and so, naturally, he won, married the princess, and lived happily ever after in the magic kingdom.

Ameera stopped singing to listen. She thought, *I bet I could plow that field even faster! But what if I don't want to marry anyone? What would I get for a prize?*

What do you think Ameera would *want* for a prize? Well, I will tell you—she would want to live in the kingdom with Big Sister, the dog, the cat, the parrot, and all the other animals, of course. What a life they would have! Strolling in fragrant flower gardens and having fancy feasts every day! Ameera would sing to her heart's content, and no one would ever tell her to stop and listen to a lesson. She and Big Sister would never have to do another chore again. Everything would be done magically for them.

After story time her class went outside for recess. Ameera started singing again, this time loud enough so that the other kids could hear. They all gathered round, and when she was done, they clapped.

"What a pretty voice you have," Lionel said.

"What a pretty song you sing," Charlotta said.

"So elegant," Ursula said.

"So cheerful," Evelyn said.

"And so comforting," Rodney said.

"You're so talented," said Emmett.

"*I* want to be a famous singer," Lindalee said.

"Me too!" Hans agreed.

"Chee-chee-chee!" Mateo said.

Bob just nodded.

They begged Ameera to sing another song, and so she did. There were no words in this song, but it was even lovelier—full of *la-la*s and *da-da*s and *dum-dee-dum*s.

After school, Ameera sang all the way home. When she got there, Big Sister was on the roof with a hammer and nails, and she was not happy.

You see, while Ameera had been in school, a tornado had blown the roof off their house.

"Stop that singing and help me nail these shingles back on!" Big Sister shouted. "This roof won't get fixed by magic."

Ameera tried to stop singing, but she couldn't!
The singing kept pouring out of her.

Dum-dee-dee-dum-dee,
la-la-dee-da-la,
doo-doo-dum-dee-doo,
la-da-da-la-da-lee-lee,
La-la-la-la-la-la-la-la-la-la . . . !

"STOP it!" Big Sister shouted.

Ameera tried to shut her mouth tight, but it stayed open, and the *la-la-la*s kept coming.

Ameera went to the barn to get another ladder, singing all the way. The dog followed her. First the dog was barking, "Woof, woof!" But then a funny thing happened. The barking turned into singing. *Woof-la-la-la-la!*

Ameera got a hammer. The cat followed her, behind the dog. The cat meowed, "Mew, mew!" But

guess what? The cat's meow turned into singing.
Mew-la-la-la!

And then Ameera got a box of nails and the
parrot came flying after her, behind the cat and
the dog. The parrot was chirping, "Tweet, tweet!"
But, you guessed it, soon the tweets turned into
Tweet-la-la-la-la!

So now there was a chorus—Ameera, the dog,
the cat, and the parrot, all singing *la-la-la.*

Then along came the one horse, the two cows,
the three pigs, the four goats, and the chickens.
They all joined the chorus of *la-la-las.* It was quite
the racket.

Ameera climbed up the ladder with the hammer and nails to join Big Sister. She sang the whole
time, while the animals sang below.

Do you think Big Sister was still angry? Do
you think they fixed the roof? Do you think they
ended up living in a magic kingdom like in the

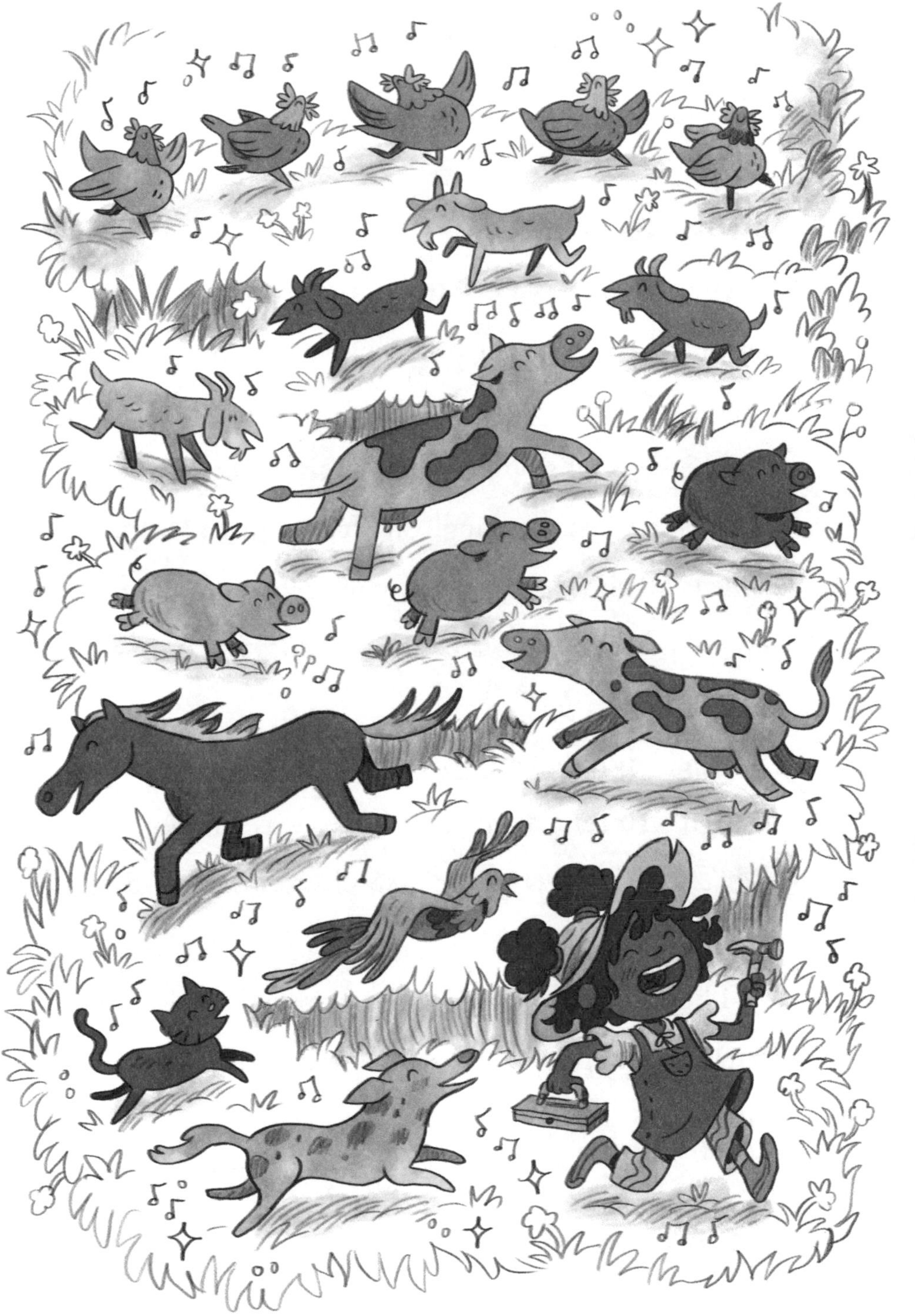

fairy tale? Do you think Ameera ever stopped singing?

I will tell you.

Big Sister was no longer angry. In fact, when she heard Ameera, the dog, the cat, and the parrot, plus the horse, the cows, the pigs, the goats, and the chickens all singing—and such a pretty song it was—she burst out laughing. It was just so funny to hear all those animals sing *la-la-la* and *dum-dee-dum*. And then Big Sister started singing, too!

La-la-la-dee-la!

They did indeed fix the roof, because even though Ameera (and everyone) was singing, it didn't mean she couldn't also climb a ladder and hammer nails.

They did not end up living in a magic kingdom—that only happens in fairy tales, and this is not a fairy tale.

And as far as that last question—did Ameera ever stop singing?

Well, no. From then on she sang all the time. Whenever she was home, the animals sang with her. Big Sister sang sometimes, too. When Ameera was in school, she sang very quietly so that the teacher wouldn't get mad and so she could learn things.

Maybe someday she will become very famous and you will get to hear her. You never can tell.

La-la-la.

The Trunk in the Attic

- THE STORY OF EMMETT -

IT WAS SATURDAY, IT WAS RAINING, AND POOR EMMETT was bored. His best friend, Mateo, was at play rehearsal; his sister, Evelyn, was practicing the piano; and his mother and father were busy, as always.

Emmett sat by the window and watched the rain pour down while he thought and thought about what to do. Finally, he got an idea! Hooray!

This was his idea: he would go to the attic and explore. (Perhaps it wasn't the *best* idea in the world, but isn't that what everyone does when they are bored, if they are lucky enough to have an attic?)

The entrance was a small square door in the

ceiling with an attached rope. Emmett got on a chair to reach the rope and pulled. The door folded down and made a rickety ladder. He carefully climbed up, squeezed through the opening, and— *ta-da!*—there he was in the attic!

It was dim and musty, just like you'd expect an attic to be. There was one tiny window. Spiders hung in their webs in the eaves. But Emmett was not afraid of spiders, so it was okay.

Now what? he wondered. Not much was up there besides the spiders and some old trunks. Emmett went to the oldest-looking one because everyone knows that the oldest trunk holds the most exciting stuff.

On top of the lid in faded red paint were the words WADDLEBEE TOY STORE.

Maybe it is full of exciting old toys! Emmett thought. He creaked open the lid and peered inside. What do you think he found?

Old toys?

No, there were no old toys.

Old books?

Nope.

And there were no old clothes, either.

There was no old anything. Too bad.

So what was in the trunk? You probably couldn't guess in a million years, so I will tell you.

There was nothing. NOTHING!

The old trunk was empty as a cracked egg.

Emmett sighed. What a dumb idea it had been to go to the attic and explore. But just as he was about to leave, he stumbled and fell into the trunk.

The lid slammed shut. *SLAM!*

And now there *was* something in the trunk. It was Emmett.

He pushed the lid from inside, but it was stuck. He banged on it and yelled, "Get me out of here!"

But everyone was busy doing busy things, and no one could hear poor Emmett yelling and banging from inside a trunk all the way up in the attic, so he stopped. What was the point? He curled up—the trunk was just big enough for that—and fell asleep.

When he woke, he was thirsty because it was so dry and hot in that trunk. Emmett sighed. And just then, a big glass of cold lemonade appeared in his hand. Imagine that! How lucky! He slurped the lemonade all down.

And then something even stranger happened. The walls of the trunk disappeared, the lid was gone, and Emmett could stand straight up.

Instead of the musty trunk walls, there were tall pine trees all around and blue sky above. Birds twittered, and the sun sparkled in between the branches. A soft breeze blew, and the air smelled earthy. Emmett was standing in a forest.

Ahead of him was a giant picnic table set with a fancy feast—little sandwiches cut into triangle shapes, all kinds of cheeses and chips and dips, plus a gigantic pile of cookies and cakes!

Emmett was hungry so he ran over to the feast. Now he could see that spiders were crawling all over everything—on the food, under the food, on the table, under the table, on the bench, under the bench, and dangling from the trees. There were big spiders, little spiders, fat spiders, skinny spiders, hairy spiders, striped spiders, spotted spiders, and more! Hundreds and thousands of spiders! Millions and billions and trillions of spiders!

Wasn't it a very, very good thing Emmett was not afraid of spiders?

One itsy-bitsy brown spider with a gold spot jumped onto Emmett's shoulder. It winked one of its eyes and pointed one of its legs to a sandwich that had no spiders on it.

So Emmett sat down and ate it.

He stayed and had a grand feast along with the spiders until every last cookie crumb was gone. You would never believe how much spiders can eat. Or how much Emmett could eat.

Then the spiders got up and started spinning and weaving webs. They crawled here and squiggled there. They zigged and zagged on their spinners from one tree to another.

The spiders worked hard and they worked fast. Emmett stood and watched, but then the itsy-bitsy brown spider with the gold spot began to spin a big web around Emmett's feet.

Emmett tried to jump out, but the spider kept spinning, faster and faster, and soon it had wrapped up Emmett's legs, then his stomach, then each arm, and finally his neck!

Oh, no!

Emmett was trapped. The spider began to spin

around his face. Strands of web got in Emmett's mouth. *Ptooey!*

Was the spider going to eat Emmett?

Do you think Emmett was scared now?

Are you?

But no, Emmett was *still* not afraid of spiders. Besides, he knew they'd already eaten a lot, so they probably weren't hungry anymore. This spider was just doing what it liked to do.

Even so, Emmett did not like being wrapped in a sticky web. He reached out and untangled himself (it wasn't that hard) and ripped apart the beautiful web that the spider had been making.

It was ruined. Poor spider!

Now Emmett felt bad. He tried to fix it. He used every one of his ten fingers and wove the strands back together.

The brown spider with the gold spot looked at Emmett with all of its eyes and clapped all of its legs.

Then Emmett and the spider started weaving together. The spider spun its threads and Emmett worked with his hands. In and around, up and down, making loop-de-loops all over the forest. Emmett was a fast weaver—he worked just as nimbly as the spider. They wove a lacy web of squiggles and spots, stripes and dots, circles and squares, and triangle pairs. Emmett couldn't remember when he'd had so much fun.

But unfortunately, fun cannot last forever. All of a sudden, there was a clap of thunder and rain poured down, and those hundreds and thousands and millions and billions and trillions of spiders scrambled off to hide. The brown one with the gold spot jumped off Emmett's shoulder and scooted away, too. Poor Emmett was left alone, getting wet.

He ran through the forest, which became walls again, and before he knew it, he was stuck in the old trunk once more. The lid was shut, and he could barely move. Ugh! He started banging.

In the meantime, Emmett's parents had stopped being busy and his sister had stopped practicing the piano. It was almost time for dinner, and they all wondered where Emmett could be.

"I'll find him," said Evelyn. She crawled up the rickety ladder to the attic, heard the banging in the trunk, and opened it.

Out came Emmett. Along with one itsy-bitsy brown spider with a gold spot.

"Look at that cute spider," Evelyn said. (Obviously, she wasn't afraid of spiders, either.)

"Thanks for letting me out," Emmett said.

As they climbed down, they saw a web of lacy lines and squiggles hanging in the eaves.

"Wow," Evelyn said in amazement.

Emmett just smiled and picked web strands out of his hair.

At the dinner table, Emmett had a very good idea. He asked his parents if he could take weaving classes.

You know what they said? Yes!

Squiggle, wiggle.

A Tiny Baby Froglet

- THE STORY OF BOB -

I HAVEN'T TOLD YOU ABOUT BOB YET, SO NOW I WILL. Bob lived across Cattywampus Street on the other side of the train tracks. The side where there was only rocks and gravel, some dirt, a few skinny trees, a muddy bog, and garbage. Do you know that side?

None of the other kids did (in fact, they didn't even know Bob—he was a mystery kid), but Bob knew it all too well. He lived there all by himself in a big brown box.

He wasn't old enough to live without parents, but as far as he knew, he didn't have any. He didn't even know what his last name was, or if he had one.

Can you imagine that? He'd lived in his box on the other side of the tracks for as long as he could remember, ever since he was a baby.

Who had taken care of him all that time?

It seemed Bob had done it all by himself. Which was fine by him, because his box was sturdy—over the years he'd added wooden planks that he found in the nearby dump and nailed on with rusty nails. His box never leaked.

And what did Bob eat? Well, he was clever and always found food that people threw out, like leftover pizza or sandwiches or crackers or oranges. Sometimes the food was a little stale, but other times it was absolutely fine.

Once he'd even found a perfect yellow banana just in front of his box. It was delicious.

Sometimes when a train sped by, Bob would stand and wave happily to the passengers. They smiled and waved back. *What a cute, brave little boy, playing all by himself by the train tracks,* they thought.

Nobody wondered why Bob wasn't in school, because he looked like a smart kid. And he was. Nobody worried that he was sad or lonely. Because he wasn't. Actually, Bob was very content with his life. Or so he thought.

One day, as Bob was eating a delicious fresh avocado (which had rolled off an avocado train just that morning right next to his box), a tiny baby frog, which in case you didn't know is called a froglet, hopped onto his lap.

"Ribbit, ribbit," the froglet ribbited.

"Hello, tiny baby froglet," said Bob. "Would you like some avocado?"

The froglet nodded, so Bob pulled off a tiny chunk of avocado with his thumb and held it out for the froglet, who gobbled it up. You see, the froglet was very hungry. It had gone on a picnic with its parents, but then they had gotten run over by a train, and the poor froglet was trying to find its way home and had not eaten in two whole days.

Bob gave the froglet another bite of avocado. And another. And another. Pretty soon there was only one bite left. Bob was hungry, too, but the froglet looked up at him and its eyes were so sad-looking that Bob said, "Here, you have the rest." He held out his hand with the last bit of avocado in it.

The froglet gobbled it down—*GULP*—in one bite.

Guess what happened next? Do you think the tiny baby froglet turned into a prince who had been magically transformed into a froglet by an evil sorcerer and needed a nice kid like Bob to offer his last bite of avocado to turn the magic around and change back into a human again in a puff of smoke? Or do you think that the froglet turned into a fairy godmother to grant Bob's wishes?

No, I am sorry to report that neither of those things happened. The last bite of avocado didn't even make the froglet talk.

The tiny baby froglet just went, "Ribbit, Ribbit," and hopped away.

Bob watched, not at all surprised, because he had never read those fairy tales about frogs that turn into princes or fairy godmothers. In fact, he had never read any fairy tales ever. Still, he was sad to see the froglet just hopping away.

You see, Bob did not get much company, and being able to share his avocado with a tiny baby froglet had made him feel good. It made him feel special. It made him feel *needed*. Things Bob had never really felt before.

Bob looked at the froglet, who was now hopping happily along the side of the tracks. Then he looked at the avocado pit. Then he looked at his box, which he'd built and lived in his entire life.

And then Bob made a decision.

He jumped up and ran after the tiny baby froglet.

The froglet saw Bob chasing him and hopped faster, but not because it was trying to escape. It was playing a game of catch-me-if-you-can with its new friend.

As Bob ran, his running turned into hopping. Soon he was hop, hop, hopping after the froglet.

Then Bob's long, human legs turned into two hind frog legs and his arms turned into two front frog legs. Bob's skin turned green, he sprouted a couple of warts, his eyes bulged out just like frog eyes, and all of a sudden—*POOF!* Bob was a tiny frog!

He wasn't quite as tiny as the tiny baby froglet, because Bob was not a baby. He was a kid. Well, actually, a former kid, because now he was a frog.

"Ribbit! Ribbit!" Bob the frog said. It was really fun to say, so he said it some more. "Ribbit! Ribbit! Ribbit!"

"Ribbit! Ribbit!" the froglet said.

Bob and the tiny baby froglet played catch-me-if-you-can all afternoon. They hopped to the muddy

bog (where frogs like to go) and splashed about and caught lots of flies with their long, grubby, groggy, froggy tongues. If you've never eaten a fly before, well, they taste pretty delicious. At least, Bob and the froglet sure thought so. Yum!

They found the froglet's many brothers and sisters and cousins and friends—who had all thought that the froglet had been run over with its parents. You can imagine how thrilled they were to see that the froglet had just been lost for a few days. They all loved meeting Bob and made him feel like a part of the family.

His entire life, Bob had thought he was happy as a kid, but this was soooooo much better.

And that is how Bob, the boy who lived on the other side of the tracks in a box, became a happy little frog living in a muddy bog.

Ribbit! Ribbit!

GHost iN tHe Toy StoRe

- THE STORY oF URSULA -

THIS IS THE LAST STORY. FINALLY! IT IS A GHoST STORY and it is scary, so if you don't like to be scared, then you shouldn't read it. If you do find yourself quaking and shaking, remember it is just a story and you can stop. You can read one of the other stories instead.

Above the Waddlebee Toy Store on Catty-wampus Street, there were two apartments. In one lived a brave and clever girl named Ursula, with her mother, her father, and her twin baby brothers, Egor and Igor.

In the other lived Mr. and Mrs. Waddlebee. They had been there since before Ursula's parents.

In fact, they had opened the Waddlebee Toy Store a long, long time ago, and Mrs. Waddlebee was the shopkeeper. That's right! The grumbly one you may have already read about.

Ursula loved visiting the Waddlebees. Well, actually, she loved visiting Mr. Waddlebee. To be honest, Mrs. Waddlebee was mean, but Mr. Waddlebee made up for it by being kind. And they always had yummy cookies.

By and by, there came the day when Mrs. Waddlebee died. She was old, and that can happen. Mr. Waddlebee built a wooden coffin and put Mrs. Waddlebee's body in it.

He said some nice things at the funeral, such as how Mrs. Waddlebee liked to twiddle her thumbs. Ursula's parents said some nice things, such as how Mrs. Waddlebee loved the store so much she would yell at anyone who came in. Egor and Igor said, "Waddley-doddley-bee!" because it was fun to say.

Now Ursula had to say something about Mrs. Waddlebee. She thought and thought. Finally, she said, "She made yummy cookies."

"Actually, *I* made the cookies," Mr. Waddlebee said kindly. "And I still will, so come over any time."

Then they all watched as the coffin was lowered into the ground and covered with dirt.

The next evening, while Ursula's father was making supper and Ursula was in charge of the twins, a big storm rolled in. The wind howled, thunder boomed, and rain poured down. Egor's and Igor's little toddler legs trembled. "Wah, wah, scary!" they cried.

"Let's get a cookie from Mr. Waddlebee," Ursula suggested. The twins stopped crying and clapped their little hands.

They all put on their shoes and headed across the hall to Mr. Waddlebee's. Ursula knocked, but there was no answer.

Where could he be in this big storm? she wondered. She creaked open the door, and she and the twins slipped inside. "Hellooo?" she called. Her voice echoed through the silent apartment.

Thunder rumbled. The twins jumped back. But there was no answer from Mr. Waddlebee. However, there was a yummy smell.

They followed the smell into the kitchen, where there was a plate of warm cookies right in the middle of the table. The cookies looked so delicious that Ursula grabbed one and bit into it.

Ow! She almost broke her tooth. It was a really hard cookie!

The twins yelled, "Cookie! Cookie!"

"Sorry," Ursula said. "These are too hard for your baby teeth." She put a cookie in her pocket anyway. Maybe it would soften up later.

The twins cried, "Wah! Wah!" Thunder went *BOOM!*, and they cried even more.

"I've got an idea!" Ursula said. "Let's go to the

toy store." She knew that toys would distract them and that the side door of the store was never locked.

"TOYS!" the twins hollered in glee, toddling back out of Mr. Waddlebee's and down the stairs, with Ursula right behind.

A wild gust of wind shook the entire building. Egor and Igor were startled for a second but then kept going—they were excited to get to the toys.

As they entered the side door, the little bell went *jing-a-ling-ling.* Ursula turned on the light, and the twins oohed and aahed and ran off to play.

Ursula headed over to a shelf of rag dolls. Which one should she play with? They all looked fun, except for one with a mean face. When Ursula moved closer, she thought she saw it twiddling its thumbs and sneering at her with its shiny pink button mouth.

Then—*BOOM! CRACK!*—thunder roared and lightning sparked. The electric light flickered, buzzed, fizzled, and went out.

"WAAH!" screamed Egor and Igor from the back of the store, and then there was silence.

It was completely dark. Ursula couldn't see a thing. She stumbled down the shadowy aisle. She walked into a cobweb. Ack. Her arm rubbed along something gooey. Eww. The floor under her feet creaked. "Egor? Igor?" she whispered.

Where oh where could they be?

All was still . . . until suddenly, a raspy voice that was definitely not the twins' echoed, "OoooOoooOooo. . . ." There was a thump like something falling. The air grew icy cold, a murky shadow flashed by, and footsteps scurried across the floor.

"Wh-who's there?" Ursula stuttered.

Bump! A ball rolled off one of the dusty top shelves—it was a magic one, because it glowed just enough for her to see Egor and Igor huddled in the corner, frozen in fear.

In front of them hovered a giant doll, faded ghostly white. Its clothes were ratted and torn, and its wild yellow yarn hair stood on end.

Ursula screamed.

If you are petrified now and want to stop reading, I wouldn't blame you. But if you like being scared, keep going. It's about to get even scarier.

As lightning flashed outside, the giant doll turned around. It glared at Ursula with piercing red eyes, then opened its pink button mouth and moaned, "Ooo-Oooo-Ooooo-OOOOOO!"

But that wasn't the scariest thing.

The scariest thing was that it held a knife, dripping in blood.

Ursula wanted to run, but she had to protect the twins, right? So she ignored her quivering insides, put her hands on her hips, stared into the doll's eyes, and demanded, "Who are you?"

"I am the ghost of Mrs. Waddlebeeeee-eee-eee," the doll howled. "Now that I am dead, no one can play in my store!" The ghost-doll loomed over Ursula. It raised the bloody knife. "Now I am going to kill YOU and your little brothers, too! Hahaha!"

Thunder boomed. The twins screamed. Ursula quaked all over. She stared at the sharp blade of the knife coming closer to her face. Closer. And closer.

Was this the end for Ursula?

She squeezed her eyes shut. She put her hand in her pocket and . . . What was that? The cookie from Mr. Waddlebee's. Ursula took it out and held it in front of her like a shield at the exact second the ghost-doll thrust the knife.

And you know what? The knife went into the cookie instead of Ursula!

You would think that would make the cookie crumble, but remember, this was a really hard cookie. In fact, the cookie was so hard that the knife broke! Hundreds of little bits of metal shattered onto the wooden floor and fell between the cracks.

The ghost-doll was aghast. It shuddered and shook, flapped its arms and spun around. With a long *hissssssss*, it twisted and shrank, then collapsed into a small pile.

Everything was quiet. Even the storm had stopped.

"Bye-bye?" the twins asked, staring at the lifeless little doll on the floor.

"I don't know," Ursula said. She touched it with the tip of her shoe. It didn't move, so she leaned down and poked it with her finger. The rag head flopped and Ursula jumped.

They all held their breath and waited, but the doll lay still. Ursula picked it up by a leg and shook it. With a final *whhhttt*, it turned to dust and vanished in the air.

The ghost was gone. Phew!

The three of them ran out the side door, up the stairs, and straight into their apartment, where they found their dinner waiting for them. And their mother and father, too!

The twins went, "Waddley-doddley-BOO!" But Ursula didn't say anything. She knew that a ghost, even though it was gone, would make her parents worry.

"Let's eat," Ursula's father said. And they did.

After supper, Ursula knocked on Mr. Waddlebee's door.

"Come in," he yawned, waking from a nap. Ursula was very happy to see him, and he was very happy to see her. He gave her a cookie. Ursula took a bite, and this time, it was soft and delicious! She ate the whole thing and took two more for the twins.

Now Mr. Waddlebee ran the toy store. He dusted off the shelves and let everyone come in and play any time they wanted. They didn't even have to buy anything. Ursula (and Egor and Igor)

and all the other kids on Cattywampus Street—
Lionel, Lindalee, Hans, Evelyn, Charlotta, Rodney,
Mateo, Ameera, Emmett, and even Bob the frog—
went whenever they could, and they all had a grand
time! And there was never, ever another ghost. At
least, not a scary one.

Ooo-Oooo-Ooooo-OOOOOO!

So It Ends . . .

I HOPE THAT YOU HAVE ENJOYED THESE STORIES, BECAUSE for now, I've told you as much as I can. If you want to know more, you'll have to go to Cattywampus Street yourself and meet up with Lionel, Lindalee, Hans, Evelyn, Charlotta, Rodney, Mateo, Ameera, Emmett, Bob, and Ursula, and they might tell you the rest. You can probably find them at the Waddlebee Toy Store or somewhere nearby.

But if you go, watch out—something odd or mysterious, silly or scary, happy or even sad might happen to you. Because while these stories may be done, yours have just begun.

Ooo-Oooo-Ooooo-OOOOOO!

Ribbit! Ribbit!

Sguiggle, wiggle.

La-la-la.

Chee-chee-chee!

Zzzzzz. . . .

Wah, wah. Woof, woof.

Boo-hoo. Boo-hoo-hoo.

Yum, yum.

Yippee!

And *jing-a-ling-ling.*

About the Author

This is a photograph of me, Lisa Jahn-Clough, when I was nine years old. Back then, I lived on a farm with my mother, father, and older brother, plus three goats, two sheep, a horse, a dog, a lot of cats, guinea pigs, two parakeets, and a monkey (yes, it's true)—all of whom I loved very much.

When I wasn't in school or doing chores, I spent time playing outside, reading, and making up stories and writing them down. Some of them were strange, funny, scary, happy, or even sad, just like the ones in this book.

Now I am much older and live in a town with a little dog named Wally, a tiny poodle named Cisco, a large cat named Willa Catter, and a person named Ed. I have written some other books besides this one. You can find out more at lisajahnclough.com.